MEET THE ROYALS

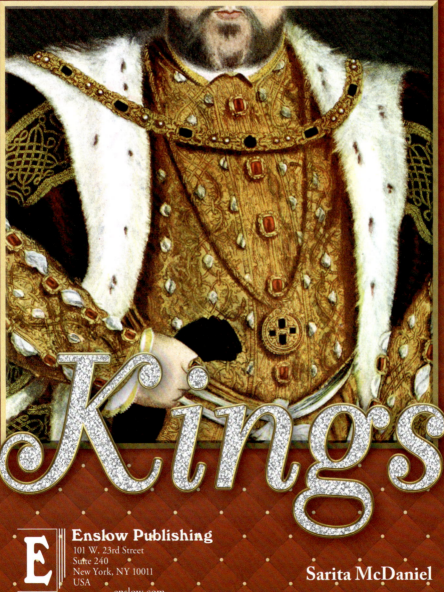

Kings

Enslow Publishing
101 W. 23rd Street
Suite 240
New York, NY 10011
USA
enslow.com

Sarita McDaniel

WORDS TO KNOW

ancient Very old.

ceremony A special event that follows a set of rules.

charity A group that works to help others.

citizen Someone who is a member of a country or other place.

coronation A ceremony to crown a new king or queen.

government The group of people who make decisions for a certain place.

inherit To pass from parent to child.

kingdom The area ruled by a monarch.

monarch A king or queen.

monarchy A country ruled by a king or queen.

rank A position in a group.

CONTENTS

WORDS TO KNOW 2

NOT JUST MAKE-BELIEVE 5

KINGS LONG AGO 7

WHAT IS A MONARCHY? 9

A NEW KING 11

WHO CAN BE CALLED KING? 13

IN CHARGE 15

SHARING POWER 17

STEPPING BACK 19

ROYAL CELEBRATION 21

STAYING FRIENDS 23

LEARN MORE 24

INDEX 24

Many fairy tales include kings and other royal people.

Not Just Make-Believe

Kings and queens are the rulers in many fairy tales. But they are not just in made-up stories. Kings and queens do rule over kingdoms. Today, there are not many **kingdoms** left.

Fast Fact

Today, 44 countries have a king or queen.

The figure in the middle is a king from ancient Egypt. Today we call him King Tut.

Kings Long Ago

The first kings ruled thousands of years ago. They were in **ancient** Iraq and Egypt. Kings had a lot of power over their kingdoms. Soon most of the world was ruled by kings.

Fast Fact

In ancient Egypt, both men and women were called kings.

The king of Morocco will pass his title to his son, the crown prince.

What Is a Monarchy?

Today, we have different kinds of **government**. Sometimes it is led by a king or queen. This is called a **monarchy**. Not just anyone can become a king. Usually, the role is passed from parent to child.

Fast Fact

"Your Majesty" is the proper way to address a king.

A new king of Tonga is crowned in 2015.

A New King

A prince is the son of a king or queen. When the prince grows up, he will become king. A **ceremony** is held. It is called a **coronation**. The new king gets his crown.

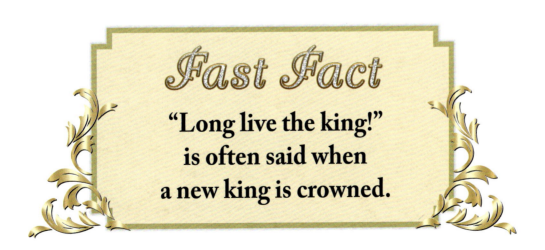

Fast Fact

"Long live the king!" is often said when a new king is crowned.

King Felipe of Spain gets married.

Who Can Be Called King?

There are different ways to become a king. In some countries, a man who marries the queen is called a king. This is not true in the United Kingdom. There, a man becomes king by **inheriting** the title.

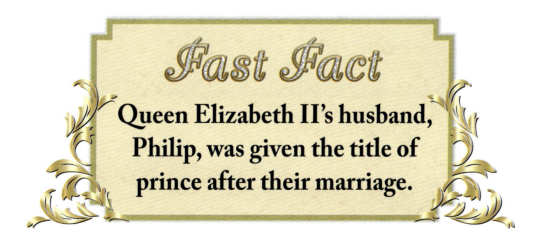

Fast Fact

Queen Elizabeth II's husband, Philip, was given the title of prince after their marriage.

King Mswati III rules Eswatini, a country in Africa.

In Charge

King is the highest **rank** in a monarchy. Some countries are still ruled by kings. In a few places, kings do not share power with anyone else in the government. These kings are called absolute **monarchs**.

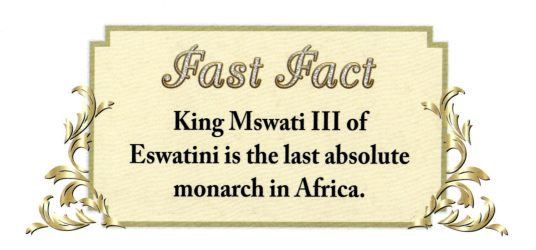

Fast Fact

King Mswati III of Eswatini is the last absolute monarch in Africa.

The king of Bhutan does not rule alone. He works with people who are elected.

Sharing Power

Today, most kings do not rule their country alone. They make decisions with the help of others. Often, a king works with a group that has been chosen by the people of the country.

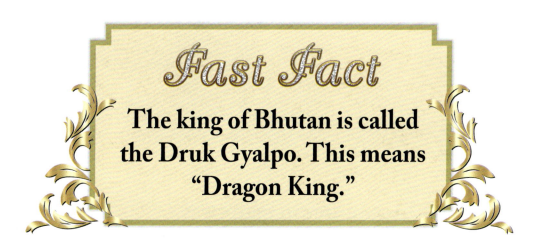

Fast Fact

The king of Bhutan is called the Druk Gyalpo. This means "Dragon King."

King Harald of Norway helps his country in many ways. He does not rule the country.

Stepping Back

Some kings have a small role in their country's government. They do not make decisions for the country. They help their countries in other ways. Many kings work with **charities**.

Fast Fact

The king's court is the group of people who give the king advice.

King Phillipe of Belgium greets his people.

Royal Celebration

Kings celebrate the good works of their **citizens**. Most kings no longer have the power they once did. But they still play important roles in their countries.

Fast Fact

Kings usually have more than one crown.

The king of Jordan meets with the American president.

Staying Friends

Kings often meet with important people from other countries. They may meet with presidents or other royals. This helps their countries stay friendly.

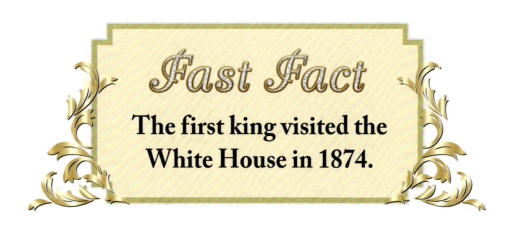

Fast Fact

The first king visited the White House in 1874.

LEARN MORE

BOOKS

DK. *Castles*. New York, NY: DK, 2019.

Lonely Planet Kids. *You Rule!: A Practical Guide to Creating Your Own Kingdom*. London, U.K.: Lonely Planet Kids, 2015.

Magyar, Caleb, and Warren Drimmer, Stephanie. *The Book of Kings*. Washington, DC: National Geographic Children's Books, 2019.

WEBSITES

The Home of the Royal Family
royal.uk
Find out more about the British royal family.

DK Find Out Kings and Queens
dkfindout.com/us/history/kings-and-queens/
Learn more about monarchs throughout history.

INDEX

Belgium, 20
Bhutan, 16
coronation, 11
crown, 11, 21
Egypt, 6, 7
Iraq, 7
Jordan, 22
kingdom, 5, 7
monarchy, 9, 15
Norway, 18
prince, 8, 11, 13
queen, 5, 9, 11, 13
Spain, 12
Tonga, 10
United Kingdom 13

Published in 2020 by Enslow Publishing, LLC
101 W. 23rd Street, Suite 240, New York, NY 10011
Copyright © 2020 by Enslow Publishing, LLC
All rights reserved.
No part of this book may be reproduced by any means without the written permission of the publisher.

Library of Congress Cataloging-in-Publication Data
Names: McDaniel, Sarita, author.
Title: Kings / Sarita McDaniel.
Description: New York : Enslow Publishing, 2020 | Series: Meet the royals | Includes bibliographical references and index. | Audience: Grades K–3.
Identifiers: LCCN 2019010204| ISBN 9781978511798 (library bound) | ISBN 9781978511774 (pbk.) | ISBN 9781978511781 (6 pack)
Subjects: LCSH: Kings and rulers—Juvenile literature.
Classification: LCC D107 .M43 2019 | DDC 321/.6—dc23
LC record available at https://lccn.loc.gov/2019010204

Printed in the United States of America

To Our Readers: We have done our best to make sure website addresses in this book were active and appropriate when we went to press. However, the author and the publisher have no control over and assume no liability for the material available on those websites or on any websites they may link to. Any comments or suggestions can be sent by e-mail customerservice@enslow.com.

Photo Credits: Cover, pp. 1, 6 Print Collector/Hulton Archive/Getty Images; p. 4 Bettmann/Getty Images; p. 8 Aurelien Meunier/Getty Images; p. 10 Edwina Pickles/Fairfax Media/Getty Images; pp. 12, 18 Getty Images; p. 14 Gianluigi Guercia/AFP/Getty Images; p. 16 Paula Bronstein/Getty Images; pp. 20, 22 AFP/Getty Images; cover, p. 1 (background), interior pages (borders) Alona Syplya/Shutterstock.com, cover and interior pages (decorative motifs) View Pixel/Shutterstock.com.